DOG TALES

Collected mainly from the oral tradition
of the Southern Appalachians

By

JOHN M. RAMSAY

Illustrations by the Author

KENTUCKE IMPRINTS   BEREA, KENTUCKY   40403

Dog Tales

COPYRIGHT©1986 BY JOHN M. RAMSAY

KENTUCKE IMPRINTS
Berea, Kentucky 40403

LIBRARY OF CONGRESS CATALOG CARD NUMBER
87-080984
ISBN 0-935680-35-7

From Grandad to:

Katey
Betsy
Mark
Luke
John
Jacob
and . . .

TABLE OF CONTENTS

PREFACE

To the author . . .
   Look at you! Going to the dogs!

To the reader . . .
   This is a fine collection that picks up the essence of tales from the Southern Appalachian oral tradition.

   Tall tales (in this case the dog tales) capture the flavor of enjoyment of the mountain people. These tales are great fun. The more ridiculous the better.

   The people of Appalachia have a delightful sense of humor, in spite of "hardships" they are able to laugh at themselves and like to share their humor with others. John Ramasay's book carries on this tradition.

   It is hoped that readers of these tales will go ahead and tell the tales, keeping alive the quality of their flavor and humor.

Richard Chase
Huntsville, Alabama
November 16, 1983

INTRODUCTION

Many reminders of pioneer times persist in Appalachia. We are about two generations closer to those times here in the highlands of southeastern United States than the flatlanders who had a more complex society, at least for the gentry. The toughness of life in the hills, where survival depended on wit, courage, and strength, fostered an independent spirit which can still confound a visiting outlander or cause a wistful longing in the eyes of a youngster who has only read about Daniel Boone.

The pioneer pursuits still have a hold on many people in Appalachia. The interest and ways of their forebears are retained, especially in the more isolated areas. One can find many young men who spend their time in the woods with a dog and gun rather than on a pair of water skis. They often prefer the education of the campfire to that of the classroom. Even whole communities may turn out for a turkey shoot but not for an evening of chamber music. Their Appalachian culture is an important part of the American story.

Good dogs, those who are well bred and well trained for trailing coon or fox, are a reminder of old times and remain a part of the living Appalachian traditions. Most of the dog tales in this collection are a legacy of this pioneer culture. The reputation of a good dog spread far and wide and entered the folklore. After all, good hounds were an important help in tracking food and soon became marketable or tradeable assets, sometimes worth thousands of dollars.

The owner of a pack of hounds will brag about his best blood, using a combination of appeal and veracity too often lacking among sophisticated Madison Avenue promoters. But it is considered foolhardy to say too much. Many mountain men and women are skilled in tailoring remarks so that a buyer gets about what he deserves.

Most of the dog tales which I have heard directly from hunters themselves have been true stories (1). Only a few such stories have been included in this collection.

When the purpose of the storyteller is to entertain, then scandalous liberties may be taken. Exaggerated tales have much more entertainment value. Such tales are often told in the first person and sound like the truth to the gullible or like some awful lie to those who cannot be deceived. A favorite pastime is to lead the unsuspecting outlander on a merry deceit.

Truth is, after all, a relative thing. When the purpose is to entertain, it can be embellished with impunity. Storytellers, at least, should follow the advice of Mike Moore, a former student of mine and a master storyteller himself: "Tell the truth; only make it sound good," he once advised some would-be storytellers!

The "truth" has additional overtones to a folklorist. It is the responsibility of a folklorist or any other scholar to be truthful. The folklorist could be expected, in recounting tales, to present an accurate chronology of events and a faithful transcript of a tale. But, a tale needs to consider not only text, but purpose, mood and all other matters which were brought into play by the tale and caused it to be told in the first place. When the pur-

1 See *Tennessee Folklore Society Bulletin* Vol XLVI No. 3, Sept. 1980, pp 75-80, for examples of true stories.

pose is to entertain, a transcription of a well-told tale may even be at cross-purposes with the needs of present listeners. That which will capture excitement in one group of listeners may not capture it in another. Faithful repetition in such a case may need be only a secondary consideration. Even a tape-recorded replay cannot recreate the original circumstances and will thus likely get a different response every time it is played. The folklorist who is trying to recreate the past is thus faced with an unresolveable dilemma.

Although past circumstances can never actually be repeated, because what is past is gone, there is also a need to recognize that the past is, in a way, continually repeated. There is precious little that is entirely new. The dilemma, a basic one in life, is what makes folk material so true to life and interesting. Much of the dilemma is a matter of semantics, man's attempt to comprehend the incomprehensible.

My mentors in these matters of folklore, the past and life are Richard (Uncle Dick) Chase, Leonard Roberts and N. F. S. Grundtvig. I have been much influenced by them and hereby gratefully acknowledge their guidance.

Uncle Dick is one of those impressive characters whose influence lasts a lifetime. He is not only a master storyteller but a knowledgeable folklorist, researcher and collector. His books, especially *The Jack Tales, The Grandfather Tales* and *American Folk Tales and Songs* established a deserved reputation for Appalachia as a land with a rich lore of tales and blessed with talented storytellers. His collection of "Jack" tales was the model which made me think that I, too, might make a collection.

But I am also indebted to Uncle Dick for the way in which he handled the folk material. He did not hesitate—well, perhaps he hesitated, but still he *did* alter the tales he heard. He adjusted, reshuffled and combined material whenever he judged such changes to improve their impact or usefulness. He repeated the past but as living material. At this he was a master and that is why his books have been so influential. He was also a careful scholar and gave credit to his sources in appended notes to his collections. I have followed his lead in these matters.

Leonard Roberts could also spin a yarn, keeping himself as well as his audience in stitches for the entire ramblings of some ancient story. Leonard introduced me to Stith Thompson's *Motif-Index of Folk Literature* and the wonderful web which links folk tales together across time, oceans, and even the barriers of language and culture. He opened my eyes to the importance of documenting material to help us unravel what the past has to teach, and to the importance of the cultural setting in trying to interpret its meaning. Leonard's first collections of tales were given verbatim, transcribed from his sources by tape recording.

Leonard Roberts was the foremost scholar of Appalachian folk tales. We are indebted to him for presenting the material he collected as nearly as he found it as was possible. Especially in *Sang Branch Settlers* has he set a new standard in the presentation of folklore. The book is a pioneer work, an attempt to make an exhaustive study of the material from one family and to present it in its cultural setting, giving, thus, as complete a picture as possible. I have not followed Leonard's lead in this, but his example has caused me to make a greater attempt to document what I have collected than I otherwise would have made.

N. F. S. Grundtvig helped me resolve the dilemma between a desire to present material as *museum pieces* or as *living tradition*. He convinced me that the printed words is "dead word," or as my friend, Kay Parke, has said, "sleeping word." Printed words are awakened only when given life by a living being. They have no worth until read and shared, usually vocally, by a living being. It is in the same way that history is dead and gone. Life alone can give meaning. Scholarship itself is never completely free from a living interpretation. In every case, the living takes precedent over the past or dead. We often forget this as we deal with matters of history. Keep this understanding in mind as you read these tales and give them the life they deserve.

What my sources have shared with me has been oral material. Oral material is living by nature and instantly responsive to each human situation. Only a few stories in this collection are from a printed source, the oral being preferred for my purposes. Kitteredge, in his introduction to the Student's Cambridge edition of *English and Scottish Popular Ballads,* reminds us that:

> . . . now and then it would be convenient if one's thoughts could disassociate literature from the written or printed page. In theory this is easy enough to do. Practically, however, it is difficult for even a professed student of linguistics to remember that a word is properly a sign made with the vocal organs, and that the written word is merely a convenient symbol standing for the word that is spoken. We are in the habit of thinking that a word should be pronounced as it is spelled, rather than that it should be spelled as it pronounced. . . History as we understand it, is the written record or even the printed volume; it is no longer the accumulated fund of tribal memories handed down from father to son in the oral tradition. . . What was once the possession of the folk as a whole, becomes the heritage of the illiterate only. . .

All of the tales in this book are best told orally and I trust that my intentions in setting them down will not be misconstrued. They are good stories worthy of being kept alive. I have not meant to "can" them and thus remove them from the "heritage of the illiterate." Read them, of course, but then become "illiterate" and recount them in your own way, and in your native tongue. In that way you will give more than the words themselves. You will give something of yourself which the printed word can only do in a very limited way. My sources shared as much with me and expect as much of you. Beware, if you live outside the South that you don't become so captivated by some of the regionalisms (which it *is* important for those who live *in* the Appalachian region to encourage) that you reject your own background and try to become a pseudo-hillbilly. We have enough of those in the comics and on TV. Be yourself, let your history become alive. Share your wit, wisdom and fantasy, and the fun which these tales can stimulate.

In publishing these stories I have tried to entertain, but only because my purposes would be thwarted if pleasure did not open the door. Folk tales, according to Richard Adams, are the collective dreams of the people (2). They touch elements and experiences which lie buried beneath the trappings of society and sometime express what is deepest in our hearts. Longings, fears, delights and despair are not easily described in other terms. We "literates" have only recently come to realize that the oral tradition is honorable, ancient and effective.

I have also hoped to provide a collection of engaging stories that are filled with good dreams. TV is giving ample opportunity for the nightmares. Some of the tales in this book could cause nightmares, I admit, but I suggest that the result depends for the most part upon the relationship between the narrator and the listener. For me, each telling has been pure joy because I have admired my friends who so personally shared their good times with me. The "boob tube" shares what it shares impersonally. It's violence is pure violence.

I have come to respect the popular and the unschooled. They are perhaps more likely to have honest dreams than the ideas of people whose responses to life have been modified by formal training.

This is rather heavy stuff with which to introduce some fun tales. My friends have become accustomed to this continuous attempt of mine to find meaning in all I do. Possibly it is be-

2 Adams, Richard. *The Unbroken Webb,* p 10

cause some of my most enjoyable moments have been attached to the "nonsense" of fantastic tales.

My first acknowledgment is to Uncle Clarence who became a childhood hero as he spun incredible tales to my brothers, sister, cousins and me when we spent those special nights supposedly sleeping in the hay mow at Hidden Paradise. I thank Uncle Clarence for making storytelling a part of my childhood. I applaud Uncle Dick Chase for paving the way in Appalachia with his *Jack Tales* and *Grandfather Tales.* I congratulate brother Leonard Roberts for coupling a love of folk material with the work of scholarship. Thanks also to all those who have shared tales with me—they are a generous lot of enjoyable folk, especially Tommy Anderson, Loyal Jones, Lewis Lamb, and students in my Folk Arts classes or in the Berea College Country Dancers troupe. My appreciation to David and Mary Littleton for counsel concerning the best use of dialect and spelling. Thanks to Oscar Rucker for his encouragement and prodding. And that special thanks which all authors understand to my friends Pamela Corley Slowkowski and Annette Singleton for undertaking work as transcriber and typist, respectively. The last thanks goes to my wife, Risse, for urging me to do the illustrations.

John M. Ramsay
112 Adams Street
Berea, KY 40403

18 August 1986

TAIL 1

THE SKINBOARD

Tommy, he had this dog. Tommy's a kinda lazy fellow, you know. He didn't like to do anything unless he had to. Got up late and sat around all evening. So, it was aggravatin' for him to go out coon-huntin' and come back in and find he didn't have a skinboard the right size. If he got him a big coon, he'd only have him a small skinboard and he'd have to stop to make a new big board to put the skin on. If he got him a little coon, why the skin board would be too big and the small skin wouldn't fit it. They's always a problem.

Now Tommy was smart even if he was lazy, and his dogs were noted for being uncommon smart. He trained them in all sorts of tricks, and jobs, too! Oh, they would roll over, and count, and even multiply. Well, he trained one of the dogs to tree coons the right size for his skinboards. He'd get out whichever skinboard was not in use for the dog to see before he ever went out for the coon. The dog would then go and get him a coon the right size to fit the skinboard.

That worked fine, except that the dog, it disappeared. And, of course, Tommy worried about him because he'd always been a faithful dog. He finally figured out what happened to him. His wife, Carolyn, had put the ironing board out on the back porch. Tommy figured the dog was probably out there still lookin' for a coon big enough to fit it.

Now, folks down there, around Brasstown, North Carolina, they scoff at that. They just didn't believe that could be the truth. They said that somebody just swiped that dog or he got killed or lost or something like that, you know. But I was telling Bill Sparks about that,—he lives out there near Paint Lick, here in Kentucky, runs the slaughterhouse—any of you know him? Plays the banjo and everything, a good fella. I was telling him about Tommy's dog. "Well, no." he says, "that dog's not lost. It was out looking for a big coon, and it heard there were some big ones up here in Kentucky. So it came up here around Paint Lick and it's got it a big coon alright; I seen it just the other day. It's got the coon penned up cause he's not quite big enough yet and he's feeding him on corn to try to make it grow a little more. Then he'll take him back to North Carolina."

TAIL 2

ON A SATURDAY ONE SPRING

Now, I told you Tommy Anderson's kind of a lazy guy and he's noted for having some pretty smart dogs. So he trained his dogs in order to where he didn't have to move a lick. If he wanted to go out and catch a ground hog, well, Tommy'd just fetch a shovel and hold it up, and that dog would go and hole up a ground hog and didn't run Tommy all over creation. If Tommy wanted a squirrel for supper, he'd just get out his squirrel rifle, hold it up and that dog'd go tree a squirrel, knew right where they's at—he'd go right to it.

Like I say, Tommy had him some smart dogs. Well, Tommy, of course now, he's just a young fellow and he's been working right hard and come a Saturday afternoon in springtime he decided it was just about time for him to take a little break. He decided it was time for him to go out fishin'—the fish ought to be bitin' right good. Well, he got his tackle box together and his pole. He got all he needed for to go fishin' and then he called for his dog.

Well, that dog didn't show up. Now that wasn't usual. Tommy, he didn't want to have to go out and hunt his dog up so he hollered again. But the dog still didn't come. Well, it takes something pretty bad like that to make Tommy mad enough to go out a-lookin' for him. He went out a-lookin' for him and I want you to know what that dog was a doin'. I told you he was a smart dog. He seen Tommy fetch his pole. Tommy found that dog out behind the house a diggin' worms. Had a whole can filled already.

TAIL 3

COOKIE

Bobby Field's dad he used to have a dog named Cookie. Little black and white hound. She followed him everywhere he went. I mean everywhere. Why, one time he was out tending to his trout lines in his boat and she just followed right along behind, paddlin' in the water.

As he went along tending his lines she got all tangled up in the trout lines and he had to go back and get her unhooked. Cookie, when she's out to the house, she used to sit by the table but when she wouldn't eat nothin' but what my dad gave her. Nothin. That's what you call loyalty.

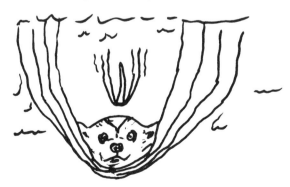

TAIL 4

THE SPIRAL CHASE

A fellow bought him a bird dog and took him out to try him out. 'Sposed to be an awful good dog, don't you know. And he started in around the field like he's on something. He went all around again. Then he went a third time and kept on goin' around and around gettin' closer and closer to the center of the field in a spiral path. Well, the fellow didn't know what was wrong with that dog and thought he must have gone plumb loco.

He's just about to pick up his gun and shoot that loco dog when it went into a point right there in the middle of the field. Well, he didn't know whether to believe that dog or not but he gave him a sign to flush. That dog, he raised up his paw and a quail flew out. Well, the fellow shot the bird and the dog he went back into a point. He didn't go and retrieve that bird. Well, the fellow gave him a sign to flush again and sure enough the dog raised his paw and another bird flew up. He shot that one too and then the dog went back into a point. Well, I want you to know he did that fourteen times before he ever quit going into a point. Then he went after them birds and brought 'em back, ever one, one at a time. Well, the fellow went over there to see what had gone on. That dog had circled around that field and herded up that covey of quail into a hole in the center of the field and trapped 'em down there with his foot on the hole and let 'em out one at a time 'cause he knew that fellow sure couldn't shoot more than one at a time.

TAIL 5

THE ACCORDION DOG

When I's a little boy I had this dog my daddy gave me. I spent all my time playing with that dog. Everywhere I went he went and everywhere he went I went. You couldn't separate us atall. He went out with me to fetch in wood, sat by the door when we ate and slept under my bed. Even went to school with me and waited by the bell rope until school was out. Now, when I started growing up, we went out huntin' together. And I found he's a pretty fast dog. Wasn't any rabbit could outrun my dog.

Well, we was comin' back in one Saturday afternoon, it was rainin' cats and dogs, and walking along the state road I was about as wet as Noah during the 40 day rain. A tourister came along driving a big black cadillac and asked me if I'd like a ride. I told him I'd sure appreciate it (It was okay back in those days to take a ride with a stranger, but I wouldn't do it today). I got in and told my dog to come in with me, we always stayed together. Now that tourister, he said, "I'll take you for a ride but I won't take your dog." So I told that tourister that was alright. My dog was fast and he could just run along outside.

So, that tourister he started up and he was going about 35 miles an hour and says, "How's your dog a doin'?" and I told him he's right outside the window doin' fine. Well, he went up to 55 miles an hour, asked me, "How's that dog a doin'?" and I told him he's right outside the window doin' fine. He then went up to 85 miles an hour on a straight stretch along the Allen's bottom land. Scared me half to death but I told him my dog was doin' fine.

Well, that man he slammed on the brakes, jumped out and ran around to my side of the car to see if I was a liar. And he seen my dog there. 'Course he didn't much look like a dog, all folded up like an accordian with his tail stickin' out his mouth.

He said, "What in tarnation?"

I told him, I said, "Mister, my dog is used to runnin' fast but he ain't used to stoppin' that quick!"

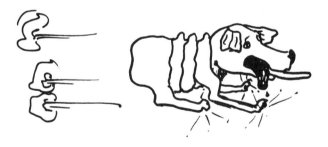

TAIL 6

WHEELCHAIR CASE

Now Charlie Lakes, he liked to go out coon huntin'. Charlie, he's from Lexington and I got this information from Brenda Russell, and she got it from Clayton Russell, who got it from his uncle.

But Charlie was out coon huntin' and they treed a coon up a white oak tree. They sawed the tree down and when it fell it split and half of it flopped over and bounced onto Charlie's dog and broke it's front legs.

Well, the men decided they'd have to shoot the dog, of course. But there's a young lad there, neighbor to Charlie and he begged for them to give him the dog. He hated to see them shoot that dog. It'd been an awful good dog, you know, good coon hunter. So they agreed, and gave the boy the dog. They never thought no more about it.

Then about three weeks later, one night, why Charlie woke up in the middle of the night and heard this dog a'barkin'. It sounded like his old coon dog on the trail of a coon. He got a light and went outside about the barn. Here this boy was with the dog in a wheel barrow, a runnin' a coon. Poor fella, that boy that is, he was plum wore out. Why, that dog liked to run coon so much that that boy had to take him out ever night. Needed a new pair of boots ever month to keep from wearing his legs off.

A SHOCKING TALE

This fella borrowed a fine huntin' dog from his neighbor. He was gonna try him out. Why, he'd hunt squirrel or rabbit, either one. The fella, he took him out huntin' and the dog was soon on on the trail of something. Then a rabbit jumped up and the fellow saw him, over in the next field. Just as he shot at the rabbit that dog ran under a 'lectric fence and his tail touched the wire. You know how an electric fence will do! He heard the shot and felt the shock at the same time. That dog thought it'd been shot. He headed for home sure that he was mortally wounded. And after that, any time anybody raised a gun, that dog would make a beeline under the house. Never was no good for huntin' ever ag'in.

TAIL 8

A COLD TRAIL

These two guys got into arguing one time about their dogs—which one could trail the coldest trail. They both had dogs who were noted for being able to follow a cold trail. So, it was decided they'd have to have a contest.

Well, they took their dogs out on the appointed day and they had to flip a coin to see which one would go first. So, the first guy, he turned his dog loose. The dog hit a trail and led the hunters to a spot where the dog sniffed around a little bit and then smelled of his paws. Then started in digging.

Well, he'd dig down aways, and then he'd smell his foot and then he'd dig some more. He went ten foot down, afore he lost the trail.

Both fellows agreed that that was pretty good. Don't you know not many dogs can trail an animal that far down, after the hole had silted up. The other hunters were ready to pronounce that dog the winner, they were so impressed.

But the second guy wasn't willing to concede. He had to give his dog a chance! So, he turned his dog loose, and his dog hit a trail and he started on through the woods. At about the end of the woods why he jumped right up in the air about four feet and ran across a field. Got to the edge of the field he jumped away up in the air again and run off into the woods.

He was really getting hot on that trail and they couldn't keep up with him. Finally he had whatever it was at bay. They could hear him sounding off way up the holler. They caught up with him after a while and I want you to know that there's a pile of big coon bones a layin' there.

So, the second fellow's dog won the bet because he'd actually found the quarry. It must have been a pretty cold trail. No tellin how long those bones had been there.

"Now, tell me." the first fellow said, "I'll concede that your dog won the bet but what's he doin' jumpin up in the air like that every once in a while?"

The second fellow said, "Well, don't you reckon that when that coon come through there they had rail fences?"

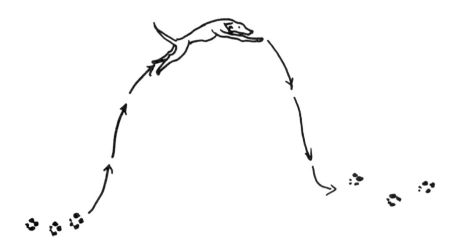

14

TAIL 9

THE DOG AND THE BUZZARD

Bill Lamb said that his folks originally had some really rich bottom land. They lived off the land, what it produced naturally. But the bottom land sort of wore out so they cleared the hills off. You know, they cleared off the hillsides and started farming on those, and started the soil washing away and down. In Georgia, this red clay soil—a drop from a drain spout will make a wash so that pretty soon the good soil is purt nigh gone.

They cropped the hills with corn and cotton, and cotton of course takes a lot out of the soil. Then the county agent came out and told them about fertilize, that they needed to fertilize their crops. So Bill's daddy went off to the big city, could of been Gainesville, and picked them up a big bag of this fish fertilize and it costs like sin too. He had to haul it home all the way on his back.

That was pretty valuable scraps. So Bill's dad told his boys, "Now, we're gonna put this stuff out careful like." He opened the sack and gave them each a teaspoon, and they measured out one teaspoon for each plant. Smelled like an overloaded fish mortuary.

His dog always guarded whatever they laid down and he told that dog, "Now I want you to keep a watch over that fertilize and don't let nothin' touch it while the boys and I are out spreading this stuff around." Well, the dog, he lay down there. Hit was a good warm afternoon, you know, summertime it was, about time to side dress the corn, and the dog went to sleep.

Well, I told you this was fish fertilize and it stinks worse'n a skunk fed on cod liver oil. The dog, it went to sleep laying down there, and this old buzzard circled round and round that dog. Bill's dad and his boys seen it circling round and round and and then watched it come down a couple yards from the dog. It seen that dog a layin' there and thought it smelled dead. So, it eased on up and pecked a big hunk out of that dog's flank!

'Course, that woke the dog up and he set up a-wailing and a-yapping most pitiful like and chased that buzzard away from there the poor bird just flapping and flapping trying to get airborne. Bill and his boys come up about then and doubled up laughing. When they came up for air and got a wiff of that fertilize in their nostrils, they doubled up again, not from laughing neither.

ROVER IN THE NANTAHALA GORGE

Karen Solesbee's grandfather trained a dog named Rover to fish for trout. He'd stick his nose in a pool of the river, find him a trout and slip it out. "My grandmother, she liked nothin' better than fresh Nantahala trout," said Karen.

Well, one winter they sent Rover out to fish and it was turnin' bitter cold, and the river was all but froze over. Rover, he got to a hole that wasn't frozen. Just about the time the dog stuck his nose in the water it froze solid. Well, he tried to bark and he whined and he shook but he couldn't get loose.

When he didn't come back why grandma she tried to get grandpa to go out and get Rover in. But he said it was too blame cold to go out. So Rover stayed out all winter long. In the spring time he thawed out, and he got him a trout and he took it up to the house, and grandma she let him in and even put a rug down for him in front of the fire so he could warm up. He finally felt fine but since that time most of the dogs in the Nantahala gorge have cold noses and prefer to stay indoors sleeping on a rug by the hearth.

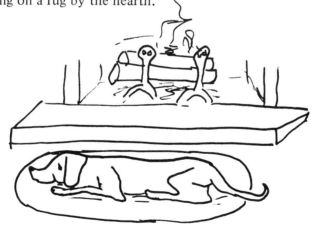

TAIL 11

SNAKE BIT

You ast why I' not here for work
    yesterday.
Well, Jake and me went up the mountain Sunday
To dig and ball up some rhododendron
For the front yard.
We brought 'em down and put 'em on
    the front porch.
Jake, he went on in to take a shower
He was mighty muddy.
Now I stayed outside putterin' around.
I looked up just in time to see
A little copperhead come outa
One a them bushes and go in the front door.
I run atter it and seen it go under the
    davenport.
I started hollerin' fer Jake.
And he come outa that shower
Mother-naked just a-drippin'.
I got him told about 'at copperhead.
Well, he got down on his hands 'n knees
A-looking under the davenport.

'Bout 'at time old Blue come boundin' in
While I 'as lookin' the other way for a stick
And he poked Jake with 'at
Old cold nose a his—
I wouldn't say where.
Jake thought he 'as snakebit.
And he fainted dead away.
Well, I turned around and seen him
And thought he 'as a goner.
I run and called the ambulance
They got there mighty quick
And got Jake in the litter-thing—
Put a blanket over him.
They got him out to the porch steps
But Jake woke up about then—right confused,
And he started out of that thing,
With them fellers a-tryin' to hold him.
Well, Jake flopped out
And he broke his leg.
That's the gospel truth.
I had to stay at the hospital yesterday
Helpin' Jake to figger it all out.

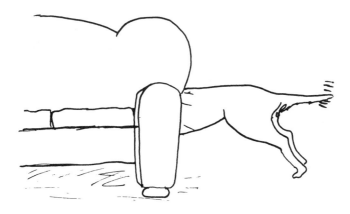

TAIL 12

OLD COLD NOSE

This farmer's chickens were disappearing and, as he slipped into bed one night, the chickens started squalling. He was really put out with losing all his chickens, he'd lost too many of them and hadn't been able to catch the varmit. So he jumped out of bed dressed in his longhandles.

He jumped out of bed, grabbed his shotgun and headed straight for the chicken house. He got out to the chicken house and bent down to undo the bolt to the chicken house door.

Well, about this time his no 'count hound dog come up behind him. Had his nose down trackin the old man and, well, he happened to run his cold nose into the opening of the seat of them longhandles where the man was bent over undoing the latch. The shock of the cold nose caused the old man to rear up just as the door come open, and the gun went off; killed ever chicken left in the coop.

I believe they said he just give up trying to raise chickens.

TAIL 13

A TAIL FROM EGON MOUNTAIN

George and his brother, well, his brother-in-law, who was Syllis King, they went coon-huntin' way back 'round about Egon, Tennessee—Egon Mountain. They had this old dog that they hadn't taken out for awhile. It was quite old, gettin' kind of senile and not getting around too well, but they thought they'd better take him out one more time.

They'd about run the other to death over the weekend, so they took the old dog out. Well, the old dog, he took off; you know, he'd been penned up for a long time and he's eager to go, so he took off and he tree'd! Boy, the way he's carrying on it sounded like it must have been an awful big coon.

Well, when they got up there, he had holed up an old wild boar under the clift. They were pretty ticked off at the dog for a false alarm, but they thought they'd have 'em a little fun and so they got a stick and poked at that wild boar and he finally broke and ran right between George's legs and turned him a flip. Didn't hurt him none.

The old dog was still a standin' there barking, but they sicked him. They wanted to find 'em a coon. And, so, the dog, why, it tree'd again and when they come up, well, it had got that same boar cornered again. They punched him out and the old hog he broke and ran right between old George's legs again and turned him a flip. George was kind of getting mad by this time.

Well, I want you to know that the dog "treed" that boar three times that night so they never did take him out coon huntin' again.

RING AND PEPPER

Now, Ring and Pepper were two dogs who were owned by a family. This is another one of those true stories.

If a sow got out of a pen, why Ring and Pepper would help put her up. Without being told they'd grab that sow by the ears, one on one side and one on the other. The family'd hear all the commotion—the pig squealing and the dogs growling as they pulled the sow by the ears. The folks would come out and tear off one of the planks in the pig pen. If the sow didn't go in why the dogs got behind her and bit her until she went in.

Somebody in the community poisoned the dogs though.

A FRESH TURNED TRAIL

Well, now this dog, another coon dog, he was after a big coon. This was about 1855. That dog was set on the coon's track, and they tracked the coon for about two or three miles through the woods and they come to a fresh plowed field. Well, of course the dog lost the scent there and so they had to go on back home.

Well, that farmer what owned the field, he raised a pretty good crop of corn on that field that year. And then plowed it again in the fall, turned it over so it'd lie fallow for the winter and of course it turned that coon track back up and so the man he came back out there with his dog and that dog went right on through that field and caught up with that coon in no time. It was a big one too, been eatin' on the corn in that field all summer.

TAIL 16

CITY SLICKER AND BIRD DOG

Bird Dog lived out in the country. He'd been out hunting and strayed some distance from home and got lost. He was trotting along the State road when this truck come along with lots of other dogs in it. This feller come out with this stick in his hand with a kind of ring on the end of it. He was right friendly like and talked nice. Bird Dog was about to ask him directions home when the man put the ring over Bird Dog's neck so that he couldn't get away and hauled him off to the big city. Bird Dog didn't know what to make of that but the other dogs in there were excited about getting a free trip to the city.

Well, when they got to the city. The man took them to a pet store. A few weeks later a man, a city slicker for sure, came into the store looking for a bird dog. Bird Dog was kind of amused at his highfalutin' talk, "My father enjoyed the sport of bird hunting. In respect to him I have come to purchase a bird dog so that I can experientially explore my heritage." So the store owner sold Bird Dog to him. Brought a good price which made Bird Dog right proud.

The city slicker also bought a pickup truck the next day and took the dog out into the country. Then unbuttoned the latch on the box in the back of the pickup, took the dog out and

pitched him up into the air. When Bird Dog fell to the ground it smarted a little bit and he let out a small yelp. Bird Dog tried to be polite, however, and when the man came over to him he looked at the man pitiful like, whined to say that he was sorry he yelped and gave a couple of wags of his tail. But instead of patting him on the head, the man picked Bird Dog up and threw him into the air again. This time, Bird Dog gave a piteous wail, then lay there howling with hurts and damaged pride. Then the city slicker picked Bird Dog up a third time and said, "I'll give you one more opportunity to catch a bird. If you fail to fly this time, I'll take you back and demand a refund." Bird Dog figured out that what country folks know by common sense ain't necessarily past on down when a family moves to the big city.

THE DEER HOUND

They had this coon dog that was bent on running deer. Now, if you know anything about dogs, you know that you don't want a coon dog that runs deer. A good coon hunt is foiled by the dog that runs off after deer, leading even good dogs astray. So, they wanted to break this dog runnin' deer. They put the dog in a barrel with rags and buck scent and rolled him down the hill. Over and over. They thought that associating that deer scent with rolling and bouncin' over the rocks would cure it. But it didn't, and next time it had a chance it was out after the deer again with all the other dogs following its lead.

Next they put skunk scent all over the dog. No one could stand being near him. Thought he wouldn't be able to smell deer through the overpowering stink of the skunk. But the dog went right on after the deer. The other dogs refused to trail at all, the skunk odor had their scent so messed up.

Well, they had to soak the deer chasing dog in a tub of tomatoes to get rid of the skunk smell. Soaked him for seven days. His hair all come out and the other dogs still couldn't stand the smell of him. But he still hunted deer.

That time the man went after the dog. He hadn't been on a good coon hunt for sometime now. He caught up with him and was about to kill him. Well, he saw that the dog had been after deer so much that he had started a'sprouting horns and his feet were growing but two toes. So he decided the dog was meant to follow the deer and he turned him loose. "I can't whup him," he said. "I'll just have to let him go and join 'em. You can't make something into something it wasn't meant to be."

TAIL 18

FASTEST DOG IN THE WORLD

Bert said he had what was probably the fastest dog in the whole world. It's a rabbit dog. He said he'd been out a huntin' one time and this dog scared up this rabbit and that dog took right off after it. Bert he shot at the rabbit but must have missed because the rabbit took off like a shot and disappeared into the woods. But he could hear the dog hot on the trail. Bert, he just stayed there, thought that rabbit'd circle around where he'd have a second shot at it.

He waited out the rest of that afternoon. Waited until plumb dark. And that rabbit never did come back. Well, Bert he gave up and whistled for his dog but that dog never did come in. Bert finally had to give in and go to the house.

Well, he got up bright and early next morning, little bit before daybreak, and went out to find his dog. He didn't want to lose his dog. Good rabbit dog. Wasn't no dog faster than her. So he went out where they scared up the rabbit and, well, directly he heard her a comin'. But you know, she was comin' from the other direction. That rabbit must have run in a mighty big circle plum around the mountain.

Directly, why, he seen that rabbit a comin'. And that dog was right behind that rabbit and I mean they was comin' fast. That

30

rabbit ran right by Bert, and that dog right behind it and I want you to know that right behind the dog was that bullet! And that bullet had a drop of sweat on it too!

TAIL 19

MAIL DOG

This fellow had a dog and he lived on one side of the mountain and his son had moved over on the other side of the mountain. The old man was gettin' pretty old and he couldn't get around too good—it was about ten miles over there so he didn't get over to see his son very often.

But he had this dog who of course knew both the old man and his son and couldn't decide which one to take up with. So the father, he decided he'd write a letter to his son and he'd attach it to the dog's neck and send a letter to his son. So he fixed it on the dog's neck and the dog took it over to the son's house. They decided that was a pretty good idea.

Now if the old man didn't write letters often enough, why that dog he'd bark at him and howl at him when it was time to go to the son's house and the old man'd have to write him another letter and send it over.

The dog's name was Bounce and he wouldn't let anyone else have the mail—just someone in the family.

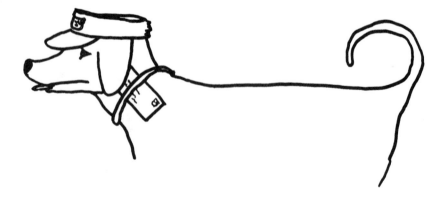

RABBIT IN THE WELL

Now, they're these two dogs, two beagles and they had never lost a rabbit. Never. But once the man who owned them had them out rabbit hunting and they quit barkin'. They're quiet. This man's friend said "Ah ha, they finally lost a rabbit."

Well, they went to find the dogs and found them. There was an old well there that had a hole in the side of it and this rabbit must have been runnin' for the hole and of course dropped in the well and those dogs hadn't lost the rabbit at all. In fact, one of them had jumped in the bucket and the other was lowering him down.

TAIL 21

COUNTING DOG

Man claimed to have the smartest dog in the country anywhere. He said he would put him up against any of 'em. And
so his neighbor who worked in a store, worked all the time,
got off from his job one weekend and he decided that he'd
borry this neighbor's dog.

So he did and this feller told him, said "Now, this dog has
got plenty of sense." Said, "Now, ever how many birds he's
got set in a covey, now he'll bark that many times."

Neighbor asked him, "Well now, will that dog do that?"

And he said, "Yes sir!"

Well, he did, he come down and borried the dog and went
out to the hills and the dog set him a covey of birds. How ever
many birds there was in there, that dog barked: fifteen, twenty,
whatever it was. Being warned like that, the feller bagged ever
one of the birds.

So he started on. The dog was way on up ahead of him,
a'goin' up a holler. Then that dog turned all at onest and come
a running just as hard as he could, come right towards that man.
I'd say the dog was kinda acting funny. Man said he didn't

know what to do with that dog, said that dog'd run up that holler and then hit would come right back. Said he'd reach down and pet the dog on the head. Said the dog wouldn't pay a bit a' attention to him. He said all at onest that dog reach't, picked up a stick and hit begin to shake that stick a'working that man on the shins with that stick 'till his shins got sore— "Why, that dog's bound to be mad!" Said, "That's all they is to it. I'm just going to kill this dog and get rid of it 'fore it attacks me." So he did. Killed the dog.

Well, he went on up the holler where the dog had went and he looked out over the lake up there and there was ducks— hundreds of 'em—thousands of ducks! So when he got back he told the man that he borried the dog from, he said, "Well, I killed ye' dog and I'm sorry. I had to do it." Said, "He went mad." Said, "I'll tell you what, that dog'd run so far and he'd come back and he grabbed a stick and next to beat my shins off shakin' that stick."

And the man what owned the dog said, "Well, why did you do that?"

Said, "I told you that dog was mad."

Said, "Noooo." Said, "That dog was trying to tell you that pond had more ducks on it than you could shake a stick at."

TAIL 22

THE BILLY ROUGH

One evening down on Fines Creek in Haywood County, North Carolina they was talkin' about their dogs, oh, kind of braggin' about which one had the best dog. Well, they decided they was no way to tell 'cept just to go out and try them out. So they agreed that they'd go out the next morning.

Next morning they went huntin' in the billy rough. You don't know what a rough is? That's a laurel thicket. It's where the bresh grows in there close together, and you can't hardly get through. There was only a bear path went through there. So they went out in the billy rough (named for Bill, I reckon) and come to a little clearing there in the laurel.

Well, they *hissed* their dogs (that's what Bobby McClure says). Well, the dogs they went out and then they come right back. The men, they didn't like that. It kind of showed 'em up.

So they *hissed* 'em again. Well, the dogs they put their tails between their legs and they didn't want to go out. Those men *hissed* 'em until finally the dogs went back out.

Well, directly they heard a racket, sounded like a devil cutting tanbark. And then everything got quiet and them dogs never come back. The men waited and waited and didn't know what that varmit was. Some old varmit must have got in a fight with them dogs.

Well, they decided they'd better go out and hunt for them. They went out in the rough and looked. It was tough going trying to get through. Never did find nary a one of them dogs. Only some hair and hide scattered around.

Well, those men decided if the varmit was that mean they'd better get out of there themselves because their lives might be on the line, too.

So they started out of the billy rough. It was getting on about dusk. Well, as they was leavin', a limb smacked that last man right on his rear end. It made him jump and he took off hollering. The next man heard him coming and thought that thing was sure right on his own heels. He took off and jumped on the back of the man in front of him. He thought that varmit had him for sure, so he took off. They all three went running out of there and they didn't stop 'til they got all the way home.

To this day, nobody hunts in the billy rough down on Fines Creek.

TAIL 23

TRAINING YOUNG FOX HOUNDS

Now, my dad, he used to train fox hounds. Did you ever wonder how they go about training them? Well, now I can tell you.

Go out and get you a young fox. Then you get you a young hound that you want to break in. Tie that fox up; tie its legs right close together where it can't get around good, then throw him down on the ground and let that dog get after it. And after a few times like that why he's got the scent of the fox, you know, and he won't ever chase nothing else.

Well, now, one time my dad was trying to train this neighbor's dog to run foxes. So we got us a young fox and tied it up while daddy held it. Then he turned the fox loose. That fox, hit just laid there. Didn't move a bit. Dad figured we must have tied it too tight so he stooped down and loosened the strings a little bit where he could get around a bit and pitched him out on the ground again. Well, the fox hit just laid there again.

Well, this was the third time and he just tied one front leg to a back leg where the fox could get around good. Well, that fox just lay there. That about beat all my dad had ever seen so he just took his knife and he cut that string.

Well, that fox it turned around and bit dad on the leg and then run into his hole. Now, I'm telling you the truth and folks down there in Madison County, North Carolina won't let dad forget it.

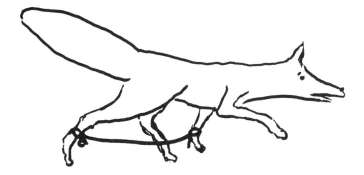

RABIES SHOTS

Well, over in Madison County, Kentucky there's a place over there, it's a *creek,* but it's called Mad *River.* And we go over there very often and go a huntin'. It was a long holler that went up from where we left our car. And every time we went up there, the dogs would get into something, we didn't know what it was at all and they would come back down the ridge in front of us, a long ridge that came back down.

We were sure it was a coon. Well, we made three trips that-away. So, one night we went and as we was a'goin' up the holler it was kindly dripping rain. And the dogs, way on ahead of us, got on the track. Well, somebody said we'd better try to cut them dogs off and keep them from going in them holes up there where they'd been after that coon. Coon might tear them up. So we did, we took the lantern and we crossed the fence and took the little branch up there and we run to the top of that hill and cut'em off where they was a big old tree up there.

At the bottom of that tree it had all rotted out 'cepting for a prong left a stickin' down in the center part of the tree. Whatever it was had run in that hole. Said, "Well, now, we have got us a coon, it went right in the bottom of that tree over there." Well, we went up there. The dogs came up and started just a barkin' as hard as they could, slobber a runnin' from their mouths, getting mad, you know, cause they couldn't catch whatever it was.

We broke out a hole in that old rotten stump. Whatever it was was down in there. We let one dog in at a time and held the others back. Well, that dog would put his head in there and ever time he'd put his head in there he'd jerk his head back right quick and the blood would fly. Thought, "Well, Lord have mercy, there's one of the biggest coons we ever got after, in all of our lives." Well, we'd hold that'n back and we'd let another'n go in. Ever' dog went in come out plumb beat.

And you know we dug back in there and hit was a fox that had the mange and hit looked just like a sheep 'at's been sheared. We got the thing out and you know we killed the miserable thing.

So we got to talking on the way home that that fox could have been a rabies fox and we'd better vaccinate our dogs. So the next morning by the peep of daylight we was in town at the drugstore a huntin' shots to give our dogs, and that's the truth, if I ever knowed it.

TAIL 25

SS–FF

They was just poor boys—it was back, you know, when times was hard. And money, money—it was very scarce. If you had thirty cents in your pocket, you thought you was a rich man. Anyway, these two boys they decided they would get them a dog. Most everybody in Kentucky had coon dogs, dogs that treed racoons, catched possum. Most of the people would eat coon or possum back then. Why, a ground hog wasn't safe 10 feet down, times was so bad.

Well, these two boys they just got aholt of an old dog—so old it couldn't hear and it weaved when it walked. You could count it's ribs from 25 or 35 foot back, you could count ever rib it had. So one of the boys was down there at the store, the little country store, and he was reading the sign on a bulletin board they had there about a great coon race they was going to have in California. He went back and told the other'n about it and he said, "It would be great to take that dog and go there."

Well, they didn't have enough money for all of 'em—to pay the dog's way and both of them, too,—their ticket up there, so they decided to scrape up what money they had and give it to one or the other'n and buy the tickets and go on up there.

So they did, took the old dog and went to the depot and bought the ticket, flipped their last penny to see who would go and so he got on there and so he went.

Well, the one who stayed here, he was anxious for to get a word back from what that dog had done. Ever day he'd go to the post office to see if he'd get a word or so from the one who

42

took the dog to California. Well, he'd been gone for about three or four weeks and well, there's a post card that come into the post office and all that was signed on it was "SS—FF."

Well, he run it through his mind, "We done real good. Why we must be rich. That's all they is to it, that's perfect there, why with all that money they's no need to be poor no more."

He figured the letter meant: Started out good, come in second, finished up in the final.

So he decided what with getting all that money his credit was good and he'd just buy him a new cadillac, buy him a new suit of clothes, get him a whole lot of cigars to have a smoke and tell all the people what they'd done out there.

Well, in three or four weeks the other boy come back, the one who took the dog out there. And he come up and I reckon he had to hitchhike to get back. He didn't have money to catch a train or nothing like that. Anyways, he come in and the one who was there said, "Now I'm glad we won that race out there, I've done got out and bought me a cadillac, a new suit of clothes and got me a whole lot o' cigars." Said, "Now you can get you something if you want to, with a part of that money."

That boy that just got back said, "No! Now we didn't win nothing."

Said, "Why? Why, you sent me a penny postal card back here and it said 'started out good, came in second, finished in the finals.' "

Said, "No, No, No. You read that wrong, it said he started, stumbled, fluted out and fell."

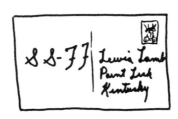

HOT ROD HOUND

Now, old man Adams, he'd been out plowin', doing his spring plowin' and he ran outa gas for his tractor. So he had to come all the way back in to the house and he got him a hose and started siphoning gasoline out of his car. Siphoned it out into a little bucket he had there.

Well, while he's a siphoning it out, the old hound dog come up and started in drinking the gas. Well, now, old man Adams he thought that dog sure enough'd get sick offa that, so he watched it. After he drank the gas, the dog started to run, and then to whirl in circles. A neighbor stopped to see what in the world was going on. The dog whirled around, around and around, faster and faster. Then all of a sudden that dog fell over like dead.

Neighbor said, "Well, Mr. Adams, what happened to your dog?"

Mr. Adams, he told him, "My dog was running along just fine but I guess he just now ran out of gas."

IN THE LEAD BY A TAIL

Now this here farmer, he was fond of his favorite dog, he was always boasting about his speed.

So, one morning, break of day, he and his friends they go out for a foxhunt. Now the dogs they all hit a trail and took off bayin' and that favorite dog was in the lead. Well, they sped over hills and across vales and the hunters a having a hard time keeping up.

Well, finally those hunters outstripped all the dogs except that lead dog and he's clean out of sight. But you can still hear that deep bark. Well, they was trying to catch up and the excitement was at fever pitch. Never had they seen a dog able to run so fast. He got plumb out of hearing.

Finally they found a woodsman a cutting timber and they stopped and asked him if he seen a fox and a dog run by.

"Yes," he said.

"How's they making it?" the hunters wanted to know.

"Well," said the woodsman, "when they come by here the dog was in the lead by a tail."

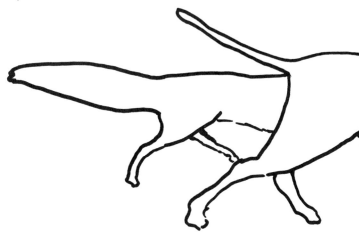

TAIL 28

QUISLING

You know that a man and his dog are great companions. A dog is man's best friend. Well, there's this old fellow. He didn't have no family. Lived by himself. All he had was this here dog. He used to talk to that dog all day long.

Well, one day while he was explainin' how unemployment could be turned from a curse into a blessing without costing the government a dime extra, the man says, "I sure wish you could talk."

And the dog says, "Well, I can."

And so they continued with their conversation, the dog agreeing with the man about a system of sabbatical leaves. The dog told the man to never tell anyone that he could talk. Well, the man went out and told his friends about his talking dog— told everyone—and brought his friends home to see the dog.

But, when he got home, I want you to know, that dog had been mauled over and killed by a whole pack of dogs that had come in the yard from all over town.

Took that man a while to figure out what had happened and I'll tell you what it was. There's a secret, probably the best kept secret in the whole world. Did you know that all dogs can talk? They can, but they don't let on like they can. Because if it were known that they could talk they'd endanger their favored position in the realm of the animal world as man's best friend!

And since that one dog had let out the secret, why those dogs had come in and killed him. 'Cause they didn't want to give up being fed, given a warm spot in the house and a pat on the head all of which they get by playing dumb.

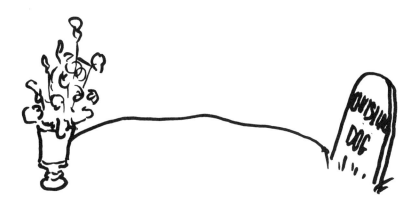

TAIL 29

ANNIE

Now up in the hills of Banks County, Georgia old Grandfather Hamilton raised hounds. His main interest was fox hunting and he and his friends often hunted Possum Ridge. They'd build 'em a fire and tip the jug a bit and tell tales.

Well, now Grandfather Hamilton, he had himself one fox hound named Annie who was the best fox hound in those parts. One night the dog ran after a fox and they went into a pasture where a man had sheep. Well, now that man that owned them was out there watchin' his sheep and he shot at the dogs.

That night the dogs all returned except Annie. Well, Grandfather, he searched Possum Ridge for two weeks to find Annie. Never did find her.

Several weeks after that they had the dogs out there running the fox again and Grandfather Hamilton heard Annie's voice out with 'em. Well, they called in their dogs but Annie wasn't amongst them. So they sent 'em out again and they heard her barkin' again.

Well, the fox turned towards the hunters. The men seen the fox comin' and that pack of hounds was behind it. There were six of them dogs after it, but the men had only taken out five dogs. Now, I want you to know that right in the lead of the pack was this white shadow of a dog that had the bark of Annie. And every night that they hunt on Possum Ridge that ghost hound will join the pack.

THE VENTRILOQUIST

Now George Vickers knew an old man that had a dog. And George was out visitin' the old man one time and got invited to supper. Now George could throw his voice. So as they was sittin' there enjoyin' the meal and the dog was sitting over there by the hearth, that dog raised up his head. He said "Ain't nobody here but the two of you, and me." Then he put his head back down. Well, that old man didn't know what to think. George was having him a time to keep a straight face. Pretty soon that dog raised up again and said "There ain't nobody here but the two of you and me, now is there?" Now, the old man he's getting kind of ancy by that then. 'Bout the third time that dog raised up his head and said "Ain't nobody here but the two of you and me, is there?" the old man's eyes got real big and he said, "Next time you say that they ain't going to be anyone here but you and George," and the old man beat it out of there.

ZIG ZAG LIPS

Well, did you ever notice that a dog's lips look like a rail fence? They're all zig zaggedy. They used to be smooth. Now, I want you to know if you go out a huntin' of course you want your dogs to bark when they get on a trail. Well, now this fellow had a dog and that dog didn't only bark on the trail, he'd bark all night long, right outside of this man's bedroom window. Well, the man he whupped him, he fired on him, he tried everything. But that dog he wouldn't shut up. So, the old man, he got fed up with that and he got that dog in and collared him good and got him a needle and thread and sewed his mouth together. Sewed it plumb shut. Well, that dog he couldn't bark no more. That old man he forgot about it the very next day and took that dog out on a hunt. When the dog got on the trail he broke ever one of them stitches loose a-barking and ever since then dog's had zig-zaggedy lips.

TAIL 32

SOUND SHOOTING BACKFIRES

Now, Sandy Howard was just about the finest man I ever knew. I looked up to him from the time I was just a little tyke. Sandy he liked to have a lot of fun, I just couldn't wait to go out with him. Anything Sandy wanted to do, I was just ready to go. But my mom, now, she wasn't so sure. When I got up to be just nearly a big teenager I wanted Sandy to let me go hunting with him.

Well, Mom and Sandy got to talking about hunting, you know, and all the times Sandy had been hunting. I had a good beagle Sandy liked to take out. I loved to hear him tell about those times. Said there were lots of things he could teach me about being careful with a gun, how to clean it, how to carry it. I could tell that mom was thinking maybe she should let him take me out with the beagle. Then Sandy told that one day while he was hunting he accidentally shot his neighbor's cow. He said he'd been up there scouting for a big buck when all of a sudden he heard this big racket in the bresh. He didn't aim to shoot at what he couldn't see. But, he'd heered about people "sound shootin." After a while he heard that rustlin' in the bresh again and he's sure it must be some big old buck. So he eased his rifle up listening for that sound, and when it came again; Kerpow! He shot it!

Well, he ran into the bresh and there lay his neighbor's cow dead as a doornail. He said that was the first and worst sound shot he'd ever made.

Well, you can imagaine my mom wouldn't let me go out a huntin' with Sandy that day. Sandy told her he's just fooling. "Course my tale was just a big joke. Never done anything like sound shooting in my life," he said. So, I asked him why he'd done it—told my mom such a big lie. Sandy said, "No fool, no fun." Well, his fooling backfired that day.

FLEA BIT

Fella had a dog that he thought was just tops. Whenever that dog barked they *was* a squirrel up that tree. Well, the weather got warm, long about black-berry pickin' time. You know the bugs, the fleas, they got pretty bad just about then.

He decided he was going a squirrel hunting and take his dog with him, get out of the house. That dog went on ahead of him up that trail in the head part of a holler, up to a tree. That dog was barkin' up there. Said, "Yeah, he's got a squirrel up that tree. I see him." So he took his muzzle-loading shot gun—back then they didn't have these up-to-date shot guns like they have now. He aimed and he shot and took the leaves off that tree, all the way to where the squirrel was at. But when he shot they wasn't a thing in the world fell. That squirrel just kept moving along the branch.

He had to reload his gun then he got down—he was an awful good marksman, they said, and he never missed. Well, that dog was right under that tree a barking. When he shot the second time not a thing fell—that thing was still a movin' up in that tree. He wanted to know what on earth was wrong.

Well, next time that he got ready to shoot, he laid down right there and got his aim, where he knowed that he wouldn't miss. And you know, he got to noticing that squirrel didn't have no tail. Then he seen it was a flea walking acrost his bushy eyebrows. When he reached up there mashed that flea, that dog never barked another lick.

HONEST SAM

Sam Clements, when he's a young fellow, he needed three dollars. Well, he was sittin' on the steps in the big city wondering' how in the world he was going to get that three dollars. As he sat there why this nice dog came along. Well, he got to a talkin' to it and pettin' it and they became pretty good friends.

A man come along down the street and he said, "Son how much will you take for your dog?"

And Sam said, "Well, now, I'll sell it to you for three dollars."

The man said, "Now that's a fair enough price, " and paid him his three dollars and took that dog along with him.

Now, Sam, he didn't like the idea of being dishonest like that so when another man came along lookin' for his dog he asked Sam, he said, "Have you seen a dog, a black and white dog, with a nice furry tail?"

And Sam said, "Yeah, I sure did."

The owner said, "Well, now I'm offering a reward of three dollars to anyone who can get my dog back."

Well, Sam went and found that fellow he had sold the dog to and gave him his three dollars back. Told him the truth, that it was someone else's dog, hit wasn't his to sell. So he took the dog, came back to its owner. The owner paid him three dollars for retrieving it. Sam was pleased to be paid for having a clear conscience.

TAIL 35

OLD HOUND DOG

There's an old hound dog and he decided that he was a gettin' up in years and all this fox huntin' and all this blood-shed, you know, and strife, and all this racket it makes, really wasn't the way to live. So he went out and made friends with the fox.

Now, his name was Old Hound Dog, and he was proud of that 'cause it has three parts to it. Old Hound Dog. His name wasn't like a lot of other names—you know, Spot, Fido, Bell or something like that. Perhaps he was part Irish and part French, he thought. Everybody knew him and they'd all say, "Look at that Old Hound Dog."

Well, once there was a group of snobbish hounds that come a huntin' for a fox. They were rather condescending to Old Hound Dog, but when they asked him about the fox, if he knew where the fox lived, Old Hound Dog said, "Yeah, I sure do." Well, those uppity hounds they scoffed at that and took to the trail. It wound around a good bit. But Old Hound Dog he just went straight to that fox's lair and waited there for those uppity hounds to come and catch up with him.

Well, the closer they come the more the hounds bayed. The closer they got up there the more racket they made. When they got there they was makin' such a racket Old Hound Dog said,

"Now just wait." He says, "Red Fox, he's in there sleeping. Just wait here and I'll go get him up." So, Old Hound Dog, went in there and barked and got the old fox up out of bed from his afternoon nap and bought him out and introduced him to all those snobbish hounds. Well, I want you to know those hounds were so amazed they never did hurt that fox. They just left there and never made a racket in those parts ever again.

NO TRESPASSING

Burt, he said he had a couple of rabbit dogs that never had failed to scare up a rabbit when they's out on the trail. Well, he had these dogs out on the trail one time and had some of his kinfolks—the menfolks—along, they was a havin' sort of a family reunion. And they's got a huntin' and those dogs they got on the trail of a rabbit.

Sounded like they's getting pretty close up to it and then all of a sudden they quit barkin' and the men never heered another sound out of 'em. Those relatives, you know how they'll do. They started in to teasing Burt and said those dogs had lost that rabbit. But Burt says, "No, I don't believe they have. They'll be right on the trail of that rabbit until they bring it around." Well, they went a looking for them in the direction they'd gone. They came to where they was a sign posted. NO TRESPASSING. So they didn't go across.

Well then, pretty soon a rabbit come skittering across the line there and the dogs followed it and they started in a barkin' again, after they crossed the line. And them dogs, they was vindicated. Burt told'em, "I told you, those dogs never lost a trail." He said, "Now when that rabbit crossed over on old man Brancher's farm there they knew that it was posted NO TRES-PASSING and they didn't want me to get in trouble so they quit barkin' till they got it back on my side."

TAIL 37

USELESS'S OLD DOG

Now I heard this on the TV . . . KET, had an interview with Useless Vanover. Now, he lives down in McCreary County and Useless had this dog that they took in the house when he got old. In the winter time, you know, it wasn't hardly fit weather for an old dog to be out.

He became a house dog. Course he helped out around the house. He used to carry blocks of wood to the fireplace and would even put 'em on the fire. But he got too old to do that after a while and he just lay there by the fireplace day in and day out. Then when it got time to put some wood on the fire why he just thumped his tail a couple of times and had them folks put the wood on so he could keep warm.

TAIL 38

THE PICKUP TRUCK

Ruby's dad had this fine coon dog. He bought him from a friend who had a big pack of dogs. Ruby's dad paid a lot of money for him. He's a pretty dog, tan and white, good breeding.

Well, the first time Ruby's dad tried him out, the dog took right off with them other dogs. You could hear him leading the pack straight away. But when the coon was treed he'd stop bayin' and head for the pickup truck, get up in the truck and take a nap. Ruby's dad didn't much like that. When a dog trees a coon why he ought to keep the coon up there. But that had set a pattern. Ever time that dog treed a coon why he'd leave the coon to the rest of the pack and head back to the pickup truck.

Ruby's dad, he tried to break the dog's habit. He blindfolded that dog before he took him out but it still didn't do no good. He would find that old pickup every time. Bought him a new pickup truck and didn't let the dog see the truck. Crated the blindfolded dog and, carted that crate on his back up the mountain before he turned the dog loose.

Well, that time the dogs treed a coon but that lead dog headed out for the truck. When Ruby's dad got back to the truck that dog wasn't anywhere to be seen. The dog didn't know the new truck, he just knew the old one. Man thought, he'd lost that dog—hated to lose him after paying all that money for him.

But Ruby's dad he was in town next day and he was walking down by that used car lot where he'd traded for that new pickup truck. His old pickup was still sittin' there in the lot. As he went by, I want you to know, he seen that dog sittin' in that pickup.

WALKING ON WATER

There's this fellow he's an avid duck hunter. So he went out duck huntin' just every chance he got. And he had a pretty good bunch of dogs. He heard about this one dog, a retriever, that was extra special—down in Kentucky. He lived up in Ohio, so he come on down to see about this dog. The Kentucky fellow that owned the dog said, yeah, he was a pretty special dog and he didn't know whether he'd sell him or not. Said he didn't aim to let loose of him, couldn't hardly part with him. And the fellow from Ohio says, "Well, I'd like to see him work out anyhow."

So, he said, "Well, lets have a hunt together." So they arranged it and they got together one weekend, they got 'em a boat and they went out on the river where they got talking about their dogs. That Ohio fellow he had lots of money. He said, "Now, I've heered about this dog of yours all the way up in Ohio." He says, "Now, sure that you wouldn't sell him? There ain't anything that ain't got some sort of price on it."

Man said, "Well, I ain't aimin' to sell it but I reckon I might consider it if the price was right."

"Well," he says, "I'd be willing to pay $4,000 for it."

Fellow says, "Well, that could be alright, but he might be worth more than that. Why don't we wait till you try him out and then see what you're willing to pay for him?"

So they spied 'em some ducks. The ducks flew up when they started getting in close to 'em. This Kentucky fellow he shot a duck and sicced his dog out to bring the duck in. Well, the dog he went and walked across the water, picked up the duck and brought it back and dropped it in the boat. The Kentucky fellow says, "Now, what do you think of that?" He says, "How much you think my retriever's worth now?"

"Well," the Ohio fellow says, "well, I offered you $4,000 for him but I ain't gonna do it now. I sure ain't gonna pay that price for a dog that can't swim and is scared to get wet."

RIFLE TOTING MONKEY

Now, you know about this fellow had this monkey he trained to shoot? Well, see, he had these two dogs and they'd tree a coon and this fellow he'd give his monkey a gun and the monkey could climb the tree, you see, and he'd climb up the tree an' he'd shoot the coon out. Monkey couldn't stand coons at all.

Well, one time the monkey he went up the tree but he didn't shoot until he came back down and then he shot the dogs, killed 'em both.

I'll tell you what happened. That monkey, he hates coons and he'll kill them every time. But there's one thing he hates worse than a coon . . . and that's a lyin' coon hound.

MYSTERIOUS TWINS

Anna Hobbs tells me that in Possum Kingdom, near Berea, her grandmother, Maggie O'Dell, she'd sent her girl, Geneva (Anna's mother), out to the store to get some eggs. On the way home Geneva come acrost these two twin dogs and they was a fighting. Well, she dropped all the eggs, it scared her so bad, and she ran on home.

Well, her mother punished her for droppin' the eggs and said she didn't believe they was such a thing as twin dogs in a fight.

Well, one time about 10 years later, Grandmother O'Dell was on a horse and she was comin' home from the store and the horse it reared. And as it reared she saw them twin dogs in a terrible scrap and she saw they were real. She went after them with a stick. They just disappeared and she seen that they weren't no such a thing as them twin dogs. But she went home and had to apologize to her daughter for having punished her years ago. Geneva still maintains the dogs were real.

TAIL 42

RIDDLE

Do you know what time it is when you see sixteen dogs running in a pack?

Well, it's fifteen after one.

TAIL 43

LARAPIN RARAPIN SKOONKIN HUNTING

Now have you ever heard about the Larapin Rarapin Terrapin Skoonkin huntin? Well, now, Dick Chase has this in his book *Grandfather Tales* but I also heard it from one of my students in Micaville, NC back in the 50's. And it was very much like Chase had told it. Chase had collected it in Kentucky. The student might have read it in Chase's book, but he might have just heard it, too. Leonard Roberts tells the story in his book *South From Hell-fer-Sartin* and maybe you've heard Raymond McLain tell the version he learned as a young lad in the hills of eastern Kentucky from Isom Ritchie.

I went on this larapin rarapin terrapin skoonkin huntin' and so me and my Pa rounded up all the dogs, all but old Shorty, and told them we was going out on this larapin rarapin terrapin skoonkin huntin'. And all of the dogs they trailed, all but old Shorty. And then Shorty, he trailed too. And then all the dogs treed, all but old Shorty, and then he treed too.

We come up there and I clumb up that sic-eye-buc-a-moor tree, way out on a chestnut limb and sat down on a pine knot. I shook, and I shook and I shook and directly something hit the ground and I looked around and it was me!

Well, all them dogs jumped on me, all but old Shorty, and then he jumped on me, too. Now, I knocked all them dogs off me, all but old Shorty, and I grabbed him by the tail and I cut it off right up close behind his years.

Well, we come in from that larapin rarapin tarrapin skoonkin huntin' with two black eyes, four skint-up shank bones and all the dogs, all but old Shorty.

DOGHIDE SHOESTRINGS

Now, Will Mallicoat, that's Margery Mallicoat's grandfather, he told her that back in the old days he'd skinned a dog once and made him some shoestrings out of the hide. Said it was the worst thing he ever did 'cause everywhere he went why the other dogs they'd just come around and smell of his shoes and wet on him.

DOGGONE BOOTS

Doc McConnel, a one man medicine show, tells of making himself a pair of boots from a dog hide. Said they were awful good for hunting and would speed him right along when on a trail. But when he'd go to town, they proved to be a problem. Every time he'd pass a fire hydrant, one of them boots would lift his leg up.

DRUMMER JOINS THE BAND

Well, now this old man he lived up in the hills with his dog, Drummer. Now, cars couldn't get any further up the holler than the old man's house so that's where they parked right down there in front of his house. And all these teenagers they'd park there, you know, and they'd play their radios and they'd dance around and all that.

His dog, Drummer, he was kind of musical and he joined in with the teenagers. He'd dance with his tail over his back in the shape of a C note. And he played his drum now and then, too.

Well, the man saw this going on, and thought that he might make his fortune with a dog like that. He took the dog out on tour. But the dog wouldn't perform. And, the man, he just got sick of it all and he went back home.

The dog then went out on his own, and of course that's what he'd been intending to do all the time. The old man missed his dog after a while and inquired around and tried to find out whatever happened to him. He suspected what he's up to.

And he traced him from Kentucky to Cincinnati and on up to Boston where he found that he had joined the Boston Pups.

TAIL 47

THE SPLIT DOG

Had me a little dog once, was the best rabbit dog you ever saw. He was runnin' a rabbit one day, nose to the ground, and some fool had left a scythe lyin' in the grass with the blade straight up. That poor little dog ran smack into it and it split him open from the tip of his nose right straight on down his tail.

Well I saw him fall apart and I ran and as I slapped him back together, I jerked off my shirt, wrapped him up in it right quick and ran to the house with him. If you put parts back together quick enough sometimes they'll knit. I set the dog in a box and poured turpentine all over the shirt to keep the swelling down and I kept him near the stove. Set him out in the sun part of the time, too. Oh, I could see him still breathin' a little, and I hoped I wouldn't lose him. And after about three weeks I could see him trying to wiggle now and then. I let him stay bandaged another three weeks—and then one morning I heard him bark. So I started unwrappin' him and in a few minutes out he jump-ed, spry as ever.

But—don't you know!—in my excitement, blame if I hadn't put him together wrong-way-to. He had two legs up and two legs down.

Anyhow, it turned out he was twice as good a rabbit dog after that. He'd run on two legs till he got tired, and then flip over and just keep right on.

Ah Lord! That little dog could run goin' and comin', and bark at both ends.

TAIL 48

AN UNWELCOME GUEST

While the McLain family lived in Alabama where the senior McLain was Vice Chancellor of the University of Alabama at Tuscaloosa, they had a dog as an unwelcome guest one evening. An important professor was expected to supper. When Mrs. McLain met him at the door, he had a dog with him. It was a rather mangy looking critter for so fine a professor but the professor allowed the dog to come into the house with him. Not wishing to offend him, Mrs. McLain overlooked the fact that she ordinarily did not have dogs in the house, and instead took the professor's hat and coat and directed him into the living room where the dog proceeded to explore the carpet and furnishings.

His nose finally led him to the kitchen where he was underfoot as the food was brought to the table. After everyone was seated, the dog sat near the professor and looked at him with pleading eyes and cocked up ears, occasionally stopping to scratch his fleas. Finally he gave up and settled down under the table where he lay wheezing throughout the meal. The entire evening was rather strained although the McLains tried very hard to be pleasant and keep conversation friendly.

Finally the professor thanked the McLains for their hospitality, donned his hat and coat and took his leave. As he left, the dog sat in the hall watching the professor bid farewell. As the professor went out the door, Mrs. McLain asked him if he wouldn't mind taking his dog.

"My dog," the professor exclaimed, "that isn't my dog, I thought it was yours!"

TAIL 49

A BRITISH TRAIN RIDE

When Henry Besuden was a young American pilot stationed in England just after the end of World War II, he took a train from London up to the lake district for a weekend holiday. The train was crowded as it pulled out of Victoria Station and a few people were left standing in the aisle even though a rather prim looking woman had a poodle occupying the seat on the aisle side next to her own window seat. She made no move to hold the dog in her lap even when some men gave up their seats to the elderly, and to several girls trying to keep their balance on high heeled shoes, or with babes in arms. Henry, who had been sitting directly behind the woman had already given his seat to an elderly lady, who was most appreciative. He was left standing next to the poodle.

Although several of the nearby passengers sent disapproving glances toward the woman and her dog, no one ventured to ask her to hold the dog in her lap and thus free up a seat for one of the standing passengers. Henry, although reared on a fine southern plantation near Paris, Kentucky, did not have the British reserve and politely asked the woman if she would hold the dog in her lap.

"Certainly not," she replied, "Poochie deserves a seat as well as any."

None of the other passengers came to Henry's rescue. So, when the conductor came through, Henry pointed out to him that many people were standing and yet a dog was given a seat to itself. The conductor asked the woman if she would mind holding the dog.

The woman replied, "Certainly I would mind. Poochie would be humilitated to be treated like a child. She is quite well trained and grown up."

"The I must request that Poochie buy a ticket," said the conductor. The woman immediately produced two tickets a and a seat reservation for each. The conductor then told Henry that there was nothing he could do and proceeded down the aisle collecting tickets.

Passengers from other cars had crowded in seeking seats, it was a warm day and the windows were wide open. The heat in the car was getting to be more than Henry could bear since he was already hot under the collar and burning with righteous indignation. In the heat of the moment he impulsively, like many good red-blooded American men, took matters into his own hands. He picked up the poodle and tossed it out the window.

The conductor turned and said, "You know, you Americans are the funniest people, you do everything wrong. You come over here and drive on the wrong side of the road; you set your dinner table with your fork on the wrong side of the plate and hold it in your right hand, and on top of that you just threw the wrong bitch out of the window."

TAIL 50

BANJO DOG

The Morris family makes music most ever night and all weekend, too. Why, on Saturday night when most of them come home from work they'll begin about the time the peepers start peepin' if its spring or the bullfrogs commence to croakin' in summer and fall and they'll still be playing when the rooster crows. They sit out on the front porch and you can hear the music up and down the valley and even way up on the mountain.

Seems like every one of them Morrises is musical. Give one an instrument and he can play it. Sweet music, too. I've never heard any of the neighbors complain about the free concerts. In fact, many of them just naturally come by on Saturday night to say howdy and end up spending most of the night.

One Saturday night the local veterinarian had been up at the head of the hollow treating Granny Tidwell's cow who was down with milk fever and he stopped by to listen to the music and to join in the fun. Dave Morris was glad to see him and took the first chance he had between numbers to welcome the vet and to ask him to look at his old hound dog. The poor thing had a bad case of red mange. They had the dog penned up back by the woodshed and when they got there he sure enough was scratching himself right fierce with his right hind foot.

Now, the mange is not easy to cure but the vet gave Dave some medication and said he'd come back to check on him next Saturday night, if they would be making music again.

They treated that dog for three weeks but it never did any good. That dog just scratched away with his right hind foot. It looked like a permanent condition, incurable. So the vet had to give up on treatment.

"Don't fret over the dog, Dave," the vet said. "And don't be too picky. Give up trying to find a cure and buy that hound a banjo. Bet he could do right good a picking out tunes with that right hind foot!"

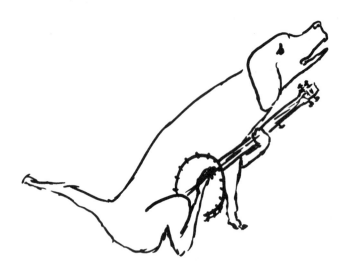

TAIL 51

THE DOG LICENSE

Loyal Jones is from Cherokee County, North Carolina. When he was a young lad he knew that he ought to have a license for his dog. So the next time he saw the dog warden he asked him how much it would cost him to get a license.

"Is your dog a male or a female?" asked the warden.

"Male," said Loyal.

"It'll be $2.00," said the warden.

"How much for females?" Loyal wanted to know.

"That's $2.00 also," said the warden. "$2.00 either way . . . don't make no difference."

TAIL 52

THE DOG TAX

Willie M. Person, an attorney of Louisburg, was one of North Carolina's most flamboyant sons. He customarily wore a flaming red vest and found joy in bizarre words and deeds. During early 1929 the impending economic collapse was casting its shadows before it, and the General Assembly was finding it difficult to raise sufficient revenues to balance the state's budget.

The State Senate, of which Person was a member, reached a section of the revenue bill which contemplated the imposition of annual taxes of one dollar and two dollars on the owners of dogs and bitches, respectively. Senator Person sent forward an amendment. As a page carried the amendment to the reading clerk's desk, the senator said, "If the legislature adopts my amendment the state's financial problems will be solved. We will not only have sufficient funds to meet all expenses, but will have a surplus in the treasury at the end of the biennium."

The reading clerk read Senator Person's amendment. It said, "Tax on male dogs, one dollar; tax on bitches, two dollars; tax on sons of bitches, five dollars."

86

THE DEAD DOG

Once I had a dog I loved. She got bad sick, so I took her in to the vet. When I got there the ride had been rough on her and the vet said that she was dead. I couldn't believe it. She'd been such a friend, understood everything I said, she was so smart. Why, I didn't even have to tell her what I was thinking.

I told the doc I had to see if she really was dead. I went out to the pick-up truck and got out that new gun I'd gotten just about the time the dog got sick. I'd been waiting a week for that dog to get well so that we could try it out. I pulled the hammer back but the dog just lay there. That wasn't good. The sound of a hammer being cocked always got her excited. I thought maybe I'd better get my old gun out, the one we'd always hunted with. Well, as soon as I cocked that old gun, my dog opened one eye, saw the gun and slapped her tail twice. The vet dosed her good then and she was ready for action the next day.

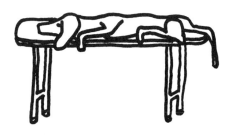

TAIL 54

THE RUNAWAY HORSES

A. D. Harrell came in with his dogs from hunting up the road toward Red Hill one afternoon. He hadn't yet let the dogs out of the trunk of the car when his eye caught sight of a neighbor boy coming down the hillside field across the valley from A. D.'s house. The boy was on a sled hitched to a couple of horses and it appeared clear in a few seconds that the horses were running wild in spite of the efforts of the boy to bring them under control.

A. D. hopped back into his car and sped down to the neighbor's house, laying on his horn to alert the boy's dad to the situation. The horses needed to be stopped before they or the lad got hurt.

No one came out of the house as A. D. pulled up in front and started calling at the top of his lungs. By this time the horses had reached the end of the lane from the field and were galloping down the road toward A. D.'s car. A. D. didn't have time to move the car even though it was also headed down the road. The horses were running so wild that A. D. figured that he'd better get out of the way himself and he backed up toward the house. He could only stand by helplessly as the horses ran into his car, one of them actually galloping right up the trunk and onto the roof before falling off and breaking its shoulder.

The horse had to be shot. A. D.'s dogs were scared to whimpering inside that car trunk but were otherwise unhurt when A. D. finally prized the trunk open and helped the dogs climb out.

THE FEUDING DOGS

Bloody Breathitt it's called. There were several feuding families and a good deal of violence among the residents, enough to match the troublous times which were regular fare for anyone trying to scrape together a living in eastern Kentucky. Jay Hatfield and Joe "Slim" McCoy were enemies in this struggle for life and some semblance of honor. They stalked each other night and day. Trained their dogs to fight each other, too.

When the men encountered each other they drew and fired . . . and missed. But it finally happened one time when Jay and Slim came out into a field at the same time, they drew and fired and . . . dead as doornails, both of them.

Uncle Fate, in the bushes, swears on a stack of Bibles that the dogs, Old Blue and Old Yaller, also met in the middle of the field and fought so fiercely that they clawed over each other climbing higher and higher until they were clean out of sight. He finally gave up waiting for them to fall back down and left to notify the families of Jay and Slim as well as the sheriff about the fight. He helped with the funeral arrangements and digging the graves.

It wasn't until a week later that Uncle Fate went back to the field to see about the dogs. There was nothing to be seen except blue and yellow hair falling from the sky.

TAIL 56

TAILIPO

We had three dogs. Their names were Youknow, Iknow and King-Queen-Calico. I had them out hunting one afternoon to try to scare up some varmit for our supper. I wasn't having any luck when the dogs finally started baying and snarling around an old fallen tree trunk. Something was in the hollow trunk and when I got there I found a big, long tail extending out of the end of the trunk. We, that is the dogs, Youknow, Iknow and King-Queen-Calico, and I pulled on that tail but couldn't dislodge that varmit. The tail was fat and furry and I figured would make a pretty good supper, so I pulled out my knife and cut it off.

Ma cooked up that tail and we all had our fill that night; even had some left over which Ma planned to put in the soup the next day. After supper we were all sitting out on the porch, quiet and satisfied after such a fine meal. Then, way off down in the woods we heard something wailing, I want my tailipoo" Scared me pretty bad and Dad told Youknow to get out there and see what it was.

Youknow left and we could hear his bark as he moved further and further into the woods, until . . . There was no more barking and Youknow didn't come back!

Then we heard it again, "I want my tailipooooooo'. . . "

We sent Iknow out. When he got about halfway through the woods he got into a terrible scrap. There was barking and screaming and terrible snarling and then . . . The barking stopped and Iknow didn't come back.

Then we heard it right at the edge of the woods nearest the house, "I WANT MY TAILIPOOOO . . . "

Dad told King-Queen-Calico to go out and get that thing. "You're the best we got," he told him. King-Queen-Calico was bristling and only waiting for Dad to send him out. We could hear a terrible fight, King-Queen-Calico really lighting into that thing and we cheered him on from the safety of the porch. Then the barking stopped. King-Queen-Calico didn't return and we had nothing to protect us.

It was pitch dark. And then we heard it right at the edge of the porch, "I WANT MY TAILIPOOOOO. . . YOU GOT MY TAILIPO!!!"

We always wondered which one of us was going to be "it" as mother grabbed someone when she said, "You," even though we'd heard her tell the tale many times.

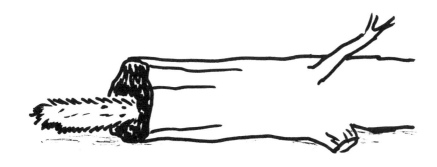

TAIL 57

ALL IN ONE BREATH

A man had 12 dogs: Hunter . . Roller . . Poler . . Toller . . Canler . . Crowner . . Bundled . . Samster . . Gilly-flowered Gamster . . Rash Rod . . Ringwood . . and Frowner.

Bill Hartsock, Berea College student, winner of the Red Foley Award and muscian with whom I've swapped caps and tales, collected this choice dog-eared tongue twister from his girlfriend's grandmother, Margy Riddel (ne: Bolling) of Flat Gap, Virginia which is not far from Pound. You are to say it all in one breath.

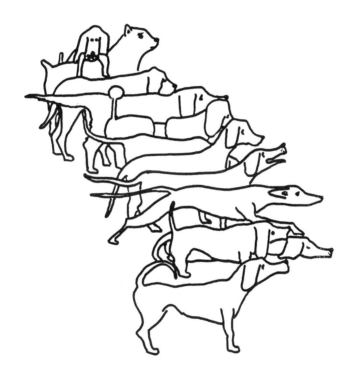

NOTES

1. THE SKINBOARD— From Tommy Anderson of Brasstown, North Carolina in 1967. The Skinboard and On A Saturday One Spring of this collection started this compiler on a search for additional dog tales. Tommy was raised in Green Cove, not far from Dog Branch. The local saying is that, "There are more Greens on Dog Branch than dogs in Green Cove."

   I have subsequently heard the Skinboard tale many times in North Carolina, Kentucky, Virginia, West Virginia and Tennessee. The epilogue about finding the dog in Kentucky was made up by Bill Sparks of Paint Lick, Kentucky about 1976 as we swapped tales enroute to a country dance engagement in Cincinnati.

2. ON A SATURDAY ONE SPRING— From Tommy Anderson (See "Skinboard"). I have not heard this tale from another source.

3. COOKIE— From Bobby Fields of Hyden, Kentucky. This is a true story. The origin of the word *trotline* is unknown although it is in common usage in the Southeast. Some dictionaries suggest a French origin. Could there have been a connection with French trappers? Or is *trotline* related to a trot-rope used to exercise horses, in which each end of the line is tied to a tree and the bridle is attached to a ring?

4. THE SPIRAL CHASE— Orginial source forgotten. H. K. (Bud) Rayfield, my wife's cousin's husband, tells this same tale, less the spiral portion. He probably heard it from Chester Cropper, on the electrical crew in Lincoln County, Missouri.

5 ACCORDION DOG— From a Berea College student in
76 and since heard in Strasburg, Virginia and a couple of
other places. My source did not liken the dog to an accordion,
that is my invention. Two friends have told me a "dirty" version, one from his childhood in Cherokee County, North Carolina in which the dog is in the car which wrecks and both dog
and its owner end up in the hospital. The owner, when he
comes to, sees the dog lying on the rug next to his bed and asks
the doctor if that is his dog. The doctor responds in the affirma-
tive to which the man says, "What's that collar thing around
his neck?" Is this the original tale? See also, Botkin, *A Treasury
of Western Folklore*, rev. ed. New York, Crown Publishers,
1975. Fay Hubbard's Dog, pp 511-512 from Idaho, *A Guide in
Word and Picture*, WPA Federal Writers' Project 1937. Also,
Botkin, *A Treasury of American Folklore* pp 533-536. Boomer
Fireman's, *Fast Lane Hound*, Crown Publishers, 1944. *Chicago
Dentist Folklore* by Jack Conroy, Manuscript for WPA Federal
Writer's Project.

6. WHEELCHAIR CASE— From Brenda Russell of Lexington,
Kentucky in 1979. Brenda got this story from her father,
Clayton Russell, who got it from his uncle, Clarence Lakes in
1976. Her story identified the boy as a "colored boy."

Curt Begley, a Berea College bus driver and a native of Berea,
gave another version. A dog would tree coons, climb the tree
to fetch them down. He had gotten three coons and was pack-
ing the fourth off a limb out over a cliff when he fell and
broke his back. The man took him out in a wheelbarrow but
the dog tried to tree three more times on the way to the vet.

An engaging version from "Decon" Hembree of Galena,
Missouri was presented in the December 1977 issue of *The
Ozark Mountaineer*.

7. A SHOCKING TALE— From Karla Thomas of Ashland, Kentucky in 1980. She learned the tale from Albert York who learned it from his father, George York.

8. A COLD TRAIL— From J. P. Fraley, Boyd County, Kentucky in 1979. I met Mr. Fraley at a May Day festival at the Hindman Settlement School in Hindman, Kentucky where Mr. Fraley was a guest fiddler. He is a well travelled mining consultant but grew up in eastern Kentucky which has a strong folk culture. Also from Marcella Morgan of Leslie County who was told it by her father, James Baker.

9. THE DOG AND THE BUZZARD— Adapted from the *Foxfire Book,* ed. by Eliot Wigginton, 1972, pp 228-229. Garden City, N. Y. Doubleday, 1972. As told by Bill Lamb. See reference for the original version.

10. ROVER IN THE NANTAHALA GORGE— From Karen Solesbee Boll of Franklin, North Carolina in 1977. Karen composed this tale as an assignment for the Folk Arts class at Berea College. It demonstrates how "creative" works draw from a base of cultural substratum. Her grandparents are from Nantahala.

11. SNAKE BIT— From Bob Terrell, columnist for the *Asheville Citizen*, daily newspaper of Asheville, North Carolina. (See also "Old Cold Nose.") This particular telling was by Loyal Jones, Director of The Appalachian Center at Berea College. He got the tale from Terrell.

12. OLD COLD NOSE— From Genevee Marlow of White Oak, Tennessee in 1979. Mrs. Marlow learned this from Lou Malicoat of Duff, Tennessee in the 1970's. The motif is widely known in differing variants. (See "Sanke Bit.")

13. A TALE FROM EGON MOUNTAIN— From Etta (Bolton) Gulley of Clairfield, Tennessee in 1979. Etta heard this story from George Malicot of Eagon, Tennessee about 1960.

14. RING AND PEPPER— From Coreen Brewer of McKee, Kentucky in 1979. Coreen learned the tale from her husband, Eugene Green of Jackson County, Kentucky somewhere about 1940. (See also "Mail Dog.")

15. A FRESH TURNED TRAIL— See Botkin, *Treasury of Western Folklore,* p 512, Rev. ed. New York, Crown Publishers, 1975. "The Smart Coon Dog," ed. by B. A. from Idaho, *A Guide in Word and Picture,* WPA Federal Writers' Project, 1937.

16. CITY SLICKER AND BIRD DOG— From Judy Hamilton in 1979. Judy, a student in the Folk Arts Class at Berea College, heard this tale from Willie Baxter of Casey County, Kentucky, I have heard the same tale from Anita Waldridge, a 1980 Folk Art student who got it from Lisa Keoku about 1971. Both girls gave this ending— "I'm going to throw him up one more time and if he don't fly, I'm gonna kill him." I felt that "I want a refund" made a better ending and also decided to tell the tale from the dog's point of view.

17. THE DEER HOUND— From Jimmy Elrod, Berea student from Washington County, Virginia in 1980. Jimmy says of this tale, "I met such a diverse number of 'characters' while growing up that I cannot pin this tale to one of them."

18. FASTEST DOG IN THE WORLD— From Bert Killian of Cherokee County, North Carolina in 1969. I swapped some dog stories with Bert while at a shape note singing at the home of Donald Ledford. Bert told this tale and "No Trespassing." I have not heard them from any other source.

19. MAIL DOG— From Coreen Brewer of Jackson County, Kentucky in 1979. Coreen learned this from her mother, Eulalia Foutch in about 1960, who learned it from her father, William Keith, of Burning Springs, Clay County, Kentucky in about 1925. She said the dog's name was Bounce. (See also "Ring and Pepper.")

20. RABBIT IN THE WELL— From Velna Key, a Berea student in 1980. Velna heard the story from her father, John Key in central North Carolina and he got it from June Peele. Velna says she "grew up hearing and sharing such tales."

    Another Berea student, Dean Rathbone (See "The Billy Rough") heard this tale from his uncle in Haywood County, North Carolina.

21. COUNTING DOG— From Lewis Lamb of Paint Lick, Kentucky in 1980. This tale is widely known and is one most likely to be told when one asks for a dog tale. Lewis' setting in the mountains is unusual and is probably his own. He is a first rate yarn spinner as well as a champion fiddler. (See "Rabies Shots" and "SS-FF.") I have transcribed his tales verbatim from tape.

22. THE BILLY ROUGH— From Dean Rathbone, a Berea student from Fines Creek in Haywood County, North Carolina, 1980. Dean learned this from his uncle, Miles Rathbone, also of Fines Creek. A recent letter from Dean says the incident really happened in the Jerry rough.

23. TRAINING YOUNG FOX HOUNDS— From Mark Rector of Madison County, North Carolina in 1981. This is a true event according to Mark.

24. RABIES SHOTS— From Lewis Lamb of Paint Lick, Kentucky in 1980. This is transcribed from Lewis' telling of a true story. (See "Counting Dog" and "SS-FF.")

25. SS-FF— From Lewis Lamb, Paint Lick, Kentucky in 1975. Lewis learned this story from a co-worker on a construction project in the Cincinnati, Ohio area back in the 40's, but in retelling changed it from horses to dogs. The tale is transcribed from Lewis' telling.

26. HOT ROD HOUND— From Sandy Coplen Smith who got it from her roommate, Susan Adams, who got it from her father in Coal City, West Virginia. I have heard the same tale several other times but the subject was a cat who was frozen in a refrigerator and revived with gasoline. This is a favorite of my grandson whose mother's father, Red Harrison of La Follette, Tennessee tells the tale.

27. IN THE LEAD BY A TAIL— See *A Treasury of Southern Folklore,* ed. by Botkin, New York, Crown Publishers, 1949. pp 128-129. Also in *The Old Time Tennessee Orator* by John Randall, pp 359-360.

28. QUISLING— From Gwen McVicker in 1980, who has it from Andy McMahan of Louisville, Kentucky. David Macemon of Woodford County, Kentucky says he has heard a Science Fiction story about Thomas A. Edison inventing an intelligence test which he tries on a dog who scores "way off the top." The dog then admits that he can talk and is killed by other dogs for giving out the secret.

29. ANNIE— From Marshall Roberts, a Berea College student in 1981, who heard the story from Alan Tench of Banks County, Georgia, who had it from his grandfather, Hamilton Tench.

30. THE VENTRILOQUIST— I failed to note where I first heard this tale. It is fairly widespread.

31. ZIG ZAG LIPS— From Johnson, F. Roy, *How and Why*, Johnson Publishing Company, Murfreesboro, NC, 1971. Source was T. K. Warren of Hereford County, North Carolina in 1966. Used by permission from author.

32. SOUND SHOOTING BACKFIRES— From a Berea College student.

33. FLEA BIT— From Lewis Lamb, transcription of taping in 1980. (See also "Rabies Shots" and "SS-FF" and "Counting Dog.")

34. HONEST SAM— This rendition is quite different from Mark Twain's original story. See *The Autobiography of Mark Twain* ed. by Charles Neider, Harper & Row, New York, 1959, pp 155-159.

35. OLD HOUND DOG— From Mona Coleman in 1976, Berea College.

36. NO TRESPASSING— From Bert Killian, Murphy, North Carolina 1969. (See also "Fastest Dog in the World.")

37. USELESS'S OLD DOG— From Kentucky Educational Television program of a video tape interview with Ulysses (pronounced useless) Vanover of McCreary County, Kentucky and aired January 5, 1977.

38. THE PICKUP TRUCK— Composed by Ruby Altizer, Berea College student in 1977.

39. WALKING ON WATER— From Loyal Jones, Director of the Berea College Appalachian Center, 1975. This is one of the most widespread dog stories.

40. RIFLE TOTING MONKEY— From Loyal Jones (See "Walking on Water") and Michael Doane Moore in 1978. Jerry Clower's humor and stories have had a widespread audience and much of his material has entered the folk process. His first recording, "Jerry Clower from Yazoo City, Mississippi Talkin'" (Decca), was number 11 on national country album charts. (See article, Knock 'im out Jay-ree! in *Sports Illustrated* 38:17 pp 75-84, April 30, 1973).Clower heard the rifle toting monkey while in high school, perhaps from his cousin Johnny. Used by permission.

41. MYSTERIOUS TWINS— From Anna Hobbs, native of Madison County, Kentucky. From her grandmother Maggie Odell of Possum Kingdom in the 1970's. I checked the story out with Anna's mother, Geneva Jennings.

42. RIDDLE— From Loyal Jones (See "Walking on Water" and "Rifle Toting Monkey" and "The Dog License"), a native of Clay County, North Carolina and known all his life.

43. LARAPIN RARAPIN SKOONKIN HUNTING— Orally from a 10th grade student at Micaville School in North Carolina in 1956. Printed sources are in Roberts, *South From Hell-fer-Sartin* number 78a and Chase, *Grandfather Tales* number 15, p 137. Robert's source, Charles Holcomb on Big Leatherwood, said he heard this tale on a talking machine record when he was a boy. Chase sites an Alabama source in his compilation of *Uncle Remus.*

44. DOGHIDE SHOESTRINGS— From Marjorie Malicoat of White Oak, Tennessee in 1979. Frank Proffit, North Carolina muscian used to tell a tale about his uncle using the hide from his wife's "bitchy" dog to cover his banjo.

45. DOGGONE BOOTS— From Doc McConnel of Rogersville, Tennessee in 1984.

46. DRUMMER JOINS THE BAND— From Linda Brewer of Jackson County, Kentucky in 1978 during a Berea College Extension Course in Folk Arts. See also *Sourwood Tales* by Billy C. Clark, Putnam, New York, 1968, pp 218-224.

47. THE SPLIT DOG— By permission from Richard Chase. See Chase, *American Folk Tales and Songs,* Signet Key, 1956, pp 97-98. Chase heard it somewhere in eastern Kentucky. It appeared in *Fisher's River* (North Carolina) *Scenes and Characters* by "Skitt" published in New York, Harper & Brothers, 1859. See also Botkin, *A Treasury of American Folklore,* Bonaza Books, New York, 1954, pp 593-594.

48. AN UNWELCOME GUEST— From Beatrice McLain at Berea Christmas Country Dance School, 1979. Mrs. McLain says that *Reader's Digest* picked up the story and published it but I have not been able to find it.

49. A BRITISH TRAIN RIDE— From Henry C. Besuden, Vinewood Farm, Winchester, Kentucky in June, 1975.

50. BANJO DOG— From David Morris of West Virginia. David shared this tale during Expo-84 at the Stokely Van Camp Folklife Center in Knoxville, 1984 where he was performing during a week featuring Berea College's interest in Appalachian folk arts.

51. THE DOG LICENSE— From Loyal Jones of Berea College in 1982, (See "Walking on Water" and "Rifle Toting Monkey.") The event took place in 1960 or 1961 and was by telephone.

52. THE DOG TAX— From *Humor of a Country Lawyer*, by Sam J. Ervin, Jr. Reprinted by permission of The University of North Carolina Press, Chapel Hill, 1983, p 132.

53. THE DEAD DOG— From Joan Randall, a Berea College student who got the story from Don Sauders of North Carolina who remembers it from about 1930.

54. THE RUNAWAY HORSES— From A. D. Harrell of Tipton Hill, North Carolina. A. D. told me this tale in 1956 when I was spending an evening after testing his cows' butterfat percentage. He corroborated the tale in August 1986 and identified Edward Whitson as the lad who tried to rein the horses in.

55. THE FEUDING DOGS— From Kris Slank, Berea student who got the tale from her grandfather, K. G. McDaniel. The story has come down in the family.

56. TAILIPO— From Risse Layne Ramsay who heard it from her mother, Rilda Chandler Layne, as a child back in the late 30's. Mrs. Layne was a native of Brodhead, Kentucky.

57. ALL IN ONE BREATH— From Bill Hartsock who got it from his girlfriend's grandmother, Margy Riddell of Flat Gap, Virginia in 1982. Mrs. Riddell, born Bolling, was about age 90.

BIBLIOGRAPHY

Thompson, Stith. *Motif-index of Folk-literature.* Revised and enlarged edition. Bloomington, Indiana, University Press. 1955-58.

Thanning, Kaj. *N.F.S. Grundtvig,* Translated from the Danish by David Hohnen. København, Det Danske Selskab, 1972.

Chase, Richard. *The Jack Tales*, Boston Houghton Mifflin Co., 1943.

Chase, Richard. *Grandfather Tales*, Boston Houghton Mifflin Co., 1948.

Chase, Richard. *American Folk Tales and Songs,* New York, New American Library, 1956.

Roberts, Leonard W. *I Bought Me A Dog And Other Folk Tales From The Southern Mountains,* Berea, KY, Council of Southern Mountain Workers, 1954.

Roberts, Leonard W. *Sang Branch Settlers; Folksongs And Tales Of A Kentucky Mountain Family.* Music transcribed by C. Buell Agey. Austin, published for the American Folklore Society by The University of Texas Press, 1974.